5-Minute

Minute

Disney · PIXAR

Stories

DISNEP PRESS

Los Angeles • New York

Contents

A New Purpose

Lightning flashed across the sky as Andy ran into his room with an armful of toys, but he had accidentally left RC outside. When Andy went downstairs, Woody headed to Andy's sister's room to search for the lost toy.

Once there, Bo and Woody came up with a plan. Slinky Dog stretched his springy body out the window as Woody scrambled down his back to rescue RC.

Moments later, though, Andy's mom came to get Bo and her sheep. Andy's sister, Molly, was giving them away!

Woody snuck over to Bo as she stood in the cardboard box. He wanted to help her escape and take her back to Andy's room, but Bo was ready to go.

Years passed, and eventually a much older Andy gave his toys to a little girl named Bonnie. She loved them as much as Andy had, but things were different for Woody. He wasn't the favorite toy anymore.

When Bonnie was ready for her first day of kindergarten, Woody decided to go with her . . . just in case she needed him.

When she got upset at craft time, he came to her rescue and brought her more art supplies. Bonnie used her imagination to put them together to make a new friend . . . Forky! She even wrote her name on the bottom of his foot, just as she had with Woody.

To Woody's surprise, Forky came to life, just like the other toys.

Back in Bonnie's room, Woody introduced Forky to Bonnie's other toys.

"Bonnie made a new friend in class," he told them. "She literally *made* a new friend. Everyone, I want you to meet Forky!"

But wide-eyed Forky was *not* interested in being a toy.

"I know this is a little strange," Woody said, "but Forky is *the* most important toy to Bonnie right now."

The next morning, Bonnie and her family were going on a road trip. She loaded up the RV with her toys, including her new favorite, Forky.

One evening, Buzz Lightyear broke the news to Woody that Forky was climbing out of the moving RV. The plastic utensil jumped out the window! Woody knew he had to follow him. He couldn't leave a toy behind!

Woody found Forky, and they walked to the next town to reunite with the RV. But something caught Woody's eye in the window of an antique store—Bo's lamp!

Woody and Forky entered the store, but instead of Bo, they found a doll named Gabby Gabby. Woody introduced himself and Forky, but Gabby Gabby wasn't all that interested in Forky.

Instead, she pointed at the voice box sewn into Woody's chest. "You have what I need. Right inside there," she said.

Woody quickly escaped to the playground—but without Forky.

Before he could come up with a plan, a busload of campers overran the playground. In the middle of the mayhem, Woody spotted Bo Peep and her sheep. She was part of a group of toys that traveled around to find kids to play with.

The two friends couldn't have been happier to see each other! Bo even agreed to help rescue Forky.

Meanwhile, Buzz Lightyear had decided to search for Woody and Forky. The brave space ranger followed their trail through a carnival, but he was captured and placed on a prize wall. He met some new toys, Ducky and Bunny, who helped him escape.

Buzz found Woody and Bo, and the whole group snuck into the store to rescue Forky.

Bo pointed to a glass cabinet across the way. "That's most likely where your Forky is being kept."

Getting to it meant crossing a wide aisle that was patrolled by Dragon, the shop's tough-looking cat!

Woody knew he had to get Forky *fast*! He ran across the aisle and climbed up to the cabinet, but it was locked.

Gabby Gabby's dummies surrounded the toys and captured Bo's sheep, too. The toys escaped, but now Gabby Gabby had Forky *and* the sheep.

Bo needed to come up with a new plan. She took Woody to meet Duke Caboom—Canada's greatest stuntman. Bo thought Duke could jump across the aisle to the cabinet and rescue Forky and her sheep.

But Duke wanted no part of it. He remembered how he'd disappointed his kid when he failed to make a big jump. That was long before, and Duke hadn't jumped since.

"Be the Duke you are right now," Bo encouraged, "the one who jumps and crashes."

But Duke didn't make it! He crashed right into Dragon.

Woody urged everyone to try again to help him rescue Forky. But the toys were banged up and hurt.

Bo was upset that Woody was being so single-minded, so she led her lost toys back to the carnival.

Woody went back into the store alone
to find Forky but instead came face-to-face
with Gabby Gabby.

Woody listened as she explained how her
voice box had never worked properly and she'd
never been any kid's favorite toy.

He understood how she felt, so he gave Gabby
Gabby his voice box and got Forky back in return.

Woody's voice box was a perfect match for Gabby Gabby's record! Now it was time to find a kid for her to love, but Gabby Gabby wasn't sure any kid could love her.

"Right now," Woody said, "I'm an old rag doll that's been lost, chewed on, burned, ripped apart, thrown away, forgotten . . . who understands just one thing. I was made to help a child—any child."

Woody encouraged her to be who she really was while Bo helped find the perfect little girl for her. She found someone who was lost and needed a friend. It was a perfect match!

Woody and the other toys made their way back to Bonnie's RV. Everyone was happy to see Woody, and he was even happier to see Bonnie reunited with Forky. He had done the job he'd set out to do.

It was then he realized that there were kids and toys everywhere who would always need his help.

Woody knew that wherever he went and whichever toy he helped next, he'd always have his friends by his side.

They were partners now—to infinity and beyond.

For the Love of Racing

Cruz Ramirez and Lightning McQueen sprinted around Willys Butte. Cruz used to be a top-notch trainer of next-gen race cars, but now she was a racer and Lightning was her crew chief! They were back in Radiator Springs getting ready for her next big event.

Cruz pushed herself hard, but she got frustrated over silly mistakes.

"Ah! My tires are sliding!" she cried.

"Relax, Cruz," said Lightning. "You're doing fine."

Lightning believed in Cruz. He knew she had all the skills to be a great racer, but she was having trouble believing in herself.

"Trust you're the best and let your tires do the rest!" Lightning told her.

Cruz wanted to believe that . . . but deep down, she still wondered if she could be the best. These small mistakes were taking a big toll. She knew she could drive better than this!

As Lightning watched Cruz do laps, he could see that she was preoccupied and overcorrecting for every little slip.

Finally, Cruz pulled over.

"Why are you so tense and upset?" Lightning asked.

"I have to be perfect," she said. "I have to prove to everyone that my win at the Florida 500 wasn't just beginner's luck."

"Pushing yourself this hard isn't the answer," he said. "C'mon. Let's go get some rest."

Later, Lightning met up with Sally and Mater at Flo's.

"How's the crew-chiefin' goin'?" asked Mater.

"Tougher than I thought," Lightning replied. "Cruz is racing to prove something to the world, and I think it's holding her back."

"It sounds like she doubts her abilities," said Sally.

"Ha! That was never *your* problem, Lightnin'," Mater said. "In fact, you thought you could win all by yourself . . . till ol' Doc set you straight."

"That's it!" Lightning shouted. "Mater, you're the best!"

Early the next morning, Sally drove with Lightning to Willys Butte. The two watched Cruz do lap after lap. Lightning could see that she was still pushing herself too hard, just like the day before.

Eventually, Cruz pulled over and approached her friends. "I don't know what's wrong," she admitted.

"It seems to me you've hit a wall . . . and not the kind at a track," said Lightning. "No amount of practice laps will get you through this. In fact, overthinking it can make things worse.

"Follow us. We want to show you something."

Lightning and Sally led Cruz to the Hudson Hornet Racing Museum, which showcased mementos, posters, photos, articles, and film reels about the legendary racer.

"When Doc was in his prime, no one could touch him," Lightning said.

"He won three Piston Cups," added Sally.

Cruz looked at the trophies in awe.

"Doc loved what he did. But to him, these were just a bunch of empty cups," explained Lightning. "Nice to have, but not really important.

"Doc helped me see that real racing isn't just about winning," Lightning continued. "It's about teamwork, sportsmanship, and enjoying the thrill of doing something you love."

"I've been so focused on my mistakes, I almost forgot how much I love to race," Cruz said with a smile.

"Why don't we all go for a drive?" Sally suggested.

Sally led Lightning and Cruz on a beautiful ride through the mountains of Carburetor County. It was the same route she'd shown Lightning years before.

"It's nice to get out here and have some space to breathe, isn't it?" Sally mused.

Somewhere along the way, something shifted in Cruz.

Lightning and Sally watched how confidently and skillfully she maneuvered through the twists on the winding road.

"You're taking those turns like a champ," Lightning told Cruz.

"I'm not even thinking about technique," she said. "And it's pretty great!"

"It's all about trusting your instincts," Lightning replied.

By the time the friends returned to town, Cruz was happy and stress-free. It was clear her confidence was growing.

"This was a good day, Cruz," said Lightning. "Go get some rest, and we'll resume training tomorrow."

The next morning, Cruz woke up and found a note on her alarm clock. It read *Meet at Flo's*.

When she arrived, Cruz was surprised to see that the whole
Radiator Springs gang was there.

"We want you to know that you're part of the Radiator Springs family," said Lightning.

"We're all behind you, honey," said Flo.

"Well, shoot!" Mater added. "Of course we are. Me and Sheriff even closed a stretch of the ol' highway so you can practice somewhere new."

Cruz was touched.

But she didn't want to dart off to practice just yet. So she enjoyed a quart of oil with the gang at Flo's, then joined Luigi and Guido at Luigi's Casa Della Tires.

"I think it's time for a new set of Lightyears," Cruz said. Guido quickly put the new tires on Cruz. They looked great, and she'd never felt better!

Out on the highway, Cruz smiled at the open road ahead of her.

"Come on, Mr. McQueen," she said. "Let's race!"

Lightning and Cruz raced down the highway, fender to fender. As they approached a curve, Lightning called out, "Trust you're the best and . . ."

"Let my tires do the rest!" shouted Cruz as she whipped through the turn at top speed.

They came to a stop and looked back to see the gang cheering.

"You've got what it takes," said Lightning.

"I sure do," said Cruz. "I have the skills, a crew chief who believes in me . . . and friends who won't let me forget how much I love racing!"

Lightning smiled. "Spoken like a true race car."

THE GOOD DINOSAUR

Arlo's Birthday Adventure

Arlo was excited! The next day was the triplets' seventh birthday, and every year Momma and Poppa planned a special day away from the farm. The previous year they had gone berry picking. The year before that they had collected flowers.

Arlo shifted from foot to foot. He couldn't wait to find out what his parents had planned next.

"Well, Momma," Poppa said when he came in from the field, "would you look at these young'uns? Why, they look like they're just about old enough for an adventure!"

"Yeah!" Buck shouted. "Let's go adventurin'!"

"Where are we going, Momma?" Libby asked. "Where? Where? Where?"

Arlo gulped. An adventure? That sounded scary. Surely his parents wouldn't plan anything too scary. Would they?

Momma smiled at Libby. "We're going for a picnic by my favorite waterfall. It's where Poppa and I met, you know."

"Awww, boo!" shouted Buck. "You said we were going on an adventure. What's so exciting about an old waterfall? As the oldest, I think—"

"Only by fifteen seconds!" Arlo interrupted.

"Come now, Buck," Poppa said. "Seeing the waterfall is only part of the fun. First we have to get there. And, boy, I'll tell you, climbing to a waterfall can be quite the adventure!"

The next morning, they set off bright and early.

"We'd best get going if we want to make it to the waterfall before it gets too hot," Poppa said.

Buck and Libby groaned. They hated getting up before sunrise. But Arlo had barely slept. All night he'd been worrying about the hike. What if he got lost? What if he stepped on something and got hurt? There was a lot that could go wrong on a hike.

Arlo looked over at Momma and started to smile. She was carrying a basket of his favorite berries. Maybe the hike wouldn't be so bad after all.

It wasn't long before Arlo's belly started to grumble. "Momma, I'm hungry," he said. "Can I have some berries?"

But Momma just shook her head. "The berries are for your birthday picnic, Arlo. Come along. There will be plenty to eat when we get to the waterfall."

Arlo sighed and kept walking. It was his birthday. Why should he have to wait?

Suddenly, Arlo stopped in his tracks. He'd been so busy thinking about eating that he hadn't noticed when everything around him got darker. Without realizing it, he'd followed Momma right into a dark forest!

Up ahead, Momma, Poppa, Buck, and Libby happily continued on their way. They hadn't even noticed that Arlo wasn't with them anymore.

Arlo's eyes darted back and forth as he followed the path. Strange shadows lurked in the trees, and sharp branches poked him as he ran.

"Momma!" he shouted. "Wait up!"

By the time Arlo caught up with his family, they were climbing a
very muddy hill. Arlo looked ahead at his siblings, already in the mud,
and thought he'd had enough adventuring for the day. "Momma," he
called. "Can I have some berries now?"

But Momma shook her head again. "Not until we get to the
waterfall," she said. "Come on, Arlo. We're almost there, but be
careful. The mud is slippery."

Arlo started to climb. He hadn't taken more than three steps when something slid past him. It was Buck!

"Yahoo!" Buck shouted, sliding through the mud on his back. "This is awesome!"

At the top of the hill, Arlo could see Libby running around the trees and jumping out at Momma and Poppa. "Boo!" she shouted, making Poppa laugh.

Slowly but steadily, Arlo continued up the muddy hill.

"Come on, slowpoke," Buck called, running past him. "Last one to the waterfall doesn't get any berries!"

Arlo put his head down and continued climbing. "I can do this. At least I think I *maybe* can." He climbed a bit farther and stumbled on a rock along the way. "It's my birthday. I can do *anything* today. And I'm *not* going to let Buck eat my birthday berries!"

Finally, Arlo reached the top of the hill. He found his family staring at a giant fallen tree.

"What's wrong?" he asked.

Momma pointed at the tree. "This is the path we usually take to the waterfall, but it's blocked. We'll have to go another way."

Poppa looked around. "It looks like our only choice is across these fallen rocks. That cave there might be a dead end," he said. "Whaddaya think, Momma?"

Arlo gulped. He didn't like the idea of going into a dark cave *or* climbing over a bunch of fallen rocks.

Momma nodded. "I think you're all big enough now to handle a few fallen rocks. And besides, look at the waterfall right on the other side of them! That's the one."

"Well, then, what are we waiting for?" Poppa shouted. "Let's go!"

Poppa set off across the rocks, with Libby and Buck close behind him. Arlo went next. He slowly stepped over one rock, then another. He was going to reach that waterfall if it was the last thing he did!

But as Momma started down the path, she tripped. The basket of berries went flying, and the berries rolled into the nearby cave.

"No!" Arlo shouted. He'd gone all that way, and he was *not* going to miss eating his birthday berries. He turned around and ran straight into the dark cave.

"What happened to Arlo?" Libby asked.

"He just turned around and ran into that cave," Momma explained.

Buck looked at the dark cave. "Arlo went in there? No way."

Poppa cast a worried look at the cave. "Maybe I oughtta go in there after him."

But before Poppa could take another step, Arlo emerged from the cave. In his mouth was the basket, and it was full of berries!

"Hey, guess what!" Arlo called out. "The cave isn't a dead end. And it leads right to the waterfall!"

"I can't believe you went in there alone," Buck said.

"Weren't you scared?" Libby added.

Arlo gestured at the berries. "Well, Momma picked these berries and carried them all this way. I wasn't about to let them go to waste. Now, come on! We've got a waterfall to see."

Arlo turned around and walked back through the tunnel, and his family followed.

Poppa smiled at Momma. "It looks like our boy is growing up."

"That he is," Momma said, taking the berries from Arlo. "Now, I think it's time for that birthday picnic. And the first berries go to Arlo, for saving the day!"

Libby and Buck nodded. "Way to go, Arlo!" they cheered.

"Aaah," Arlo said as he happily munched on his berries and looked at the waterfall. "I guess some things are worth waiting for, after all."

Badge Building

Russell *loved* collecting badges. There was just one tiny problem: there weren't enough! But that was about to change.

"Okay," Campmaster Strauch began. "This is your chance to go down in Wilderness Explorer history. Each troop has been asked to submit a new Wilderness Explorer badge idea, and we'll hold a contest in two weeks. To enter, provide a description of your badge, an image of what it will look like, and proof that you have completed the work required to earn that badge."

Russell's face lit up. A chance to earn a badge that he invented himself? He *had* to win this contest!

Russell couldn't wait to get started, but he also wasn't sure what kind of badge to design.

"What do you think?" Russell asked Carl and Dug later that day. "There are so many choices. I could take care of a rescue animal or build a birdhouse or—"

Dug pushed a book over to Russell with his nose.

"Hmmm," Russell said, looking at the book. "Paleontology?"

"It means finding bones," Carl explained.

"Ooh, bones!" Dug cried, panting happily. "I know where bones are!"

Russell looked at Carl and shrugged. Paleontology *did* seem interesting.

"Okay, Dug," he said. "Paleontology it is!"

Russell started right away on his new Wilderness Explorer badge idea. First he did his research. He learned that looking for bones was called doing a dig and that the bones were called fossils. The next day, he learned what went into preparing for a dig, what tools he would need, and how scientists determined the age of the fossils they found.

Finally, he was ready to stage his own dig.

"Okay, Dug," Russell said. "Lead the way."

Dug led Russell and Carl to the local park. "Here," he said. "Find the bone! Find the bone! Find the bone!"

"Ummm . . . Dug," Russell started. "Are you sure? This is a playground."

Dug enthusiastically wagged his tail. "Bones are here. I have found the bones."

Russell still wasn't sure, but he decided to trust Dug. He and Carl carried their equipment over to a large oak tree and began to dig.

A few minutes later, Russell spotted something in the ground. "Hey!" he shouted. "Dug was right! There *are* bones here."

Russell knelt down and brushed the dirt away. Ever so carefully, he pulled the bone from the ground.

"Dug!" he said. "This isn't a fossil. This is one of *your* bones!"

Dug happily spun around in circles. "I am a good tracker. I have found the bones!"

Carl laughed. "Well, we *did* tell him we were looking for bones."

Russell sat down on a bench and put his head in his hands. "Now what am I going to do?" he asked. "I can't dig up the whole city looking for fossils."

Carl sat down next to Russell. "No, probably not," he said. "I don't think those old fussbudgets at town hall would like it if you kept digging holes in their city. Paleontology *is* a great idea for a badge, but maybe it should wait until you have the time to do it right. There must be something else you could try."

Russell knew Carl was right. He may have lost some time, but he hadn't lost his determination to win. Now he just needed to figure out a new badge.

Russell came up with idea after idea, but nothing seemed right.

Astronomy was interesting, but he didn't have time to properly track the stars.

He thought about farming or agriculture, but he couldn't raise livestock in the city. And besides, Dug had eaten all his seeds!

Russell considered building a robot, but all the robotics books were checked out of the library.

And detective work sounded exciting, but try as they might, Russell and Dug couldn't find anything to investigate!

"You know," Carl said, "maybe none of these are working because they don't mean anything to you. Is there anything you *really* want to learn more about?"

"Hmmm," Russell said, pulling a chocolate bar out of his pocket and taking a bite. "I'm not sure."

"We've never solved a mystery or built a robot. But that," Carl said, pointing at Russell's chocolate bar, "is something we *know* you are interested in."

"Mr. Fredricksen, you're a genius!" Russell cheered. "I love chocolate more than anything in the world!"

The next day, Carl picked up Russell and Dug, and the three made their way to a local bakery.

"This is Roger," Carl said, introducing Russell to the owner of the shop, who happened to be a baker and a chocolatier. "It just so happens that Roger knows everything there is to know about chocolate . . . and he owes me a favor."

Roger shook Russell's hand. Then he handed Russell and Carl their very own aprons and chefs' hats. "You'll need these," he said. "Come on back. I hope you don't mind getting a little messy!"

All morning, Roger taught Russell about making chocolate. Russell learned that chocolate started out with a cocoa bean. The bean was roasted and crushed before being mixed with things like sugar, vanilla, and milk. He even got to try mixing the ingredients together to make his own chocolate.

Then came the really fun part! Using the chocolate they had made together, Roger taught Russell, Carl, and Dug how to make all sorts of different desserts, from chocolate cupcakes with chocolate frosting to chocolate cream pie.

Even better, Russell got to taste everything as they baked.

"No chocolate for me," Dug said. "Just bones."

The next day was the contest. Russell looked around at his competition. Everyone had come up with great ideas! There was a woodworking badge, a roller coaster design badge, a moviemaking badge, and even a badge called the Night Owl. Earning that one meant staying up all night to find and identify nocturnal animals.

Finally, it was Russell's turn to present his badge.

"I call it the Chocolate Lover's badge," he said. "In order to earn it, you have to learn how chocolate is made, make your own batch, and make three different chocolate desserts."

"It certainly does look tasty!" Campmaster Strauch said.

Campmaster Strauch walked around the room looking at all the entries and then moved to the front of the room to announce the winner.

Carl put his hand on Russell's shoulder. "You did good," he said.

Next to Russell, Dug wagged his tail. "Win the badge. Win the badge," he said happily.

Russell cut into a piece of chocolate pie and took a bite. "Mmmmm, is that good!" he said. "Thank you both for helping me."

Just then, there was a cheer from across the room. The Roller Coaster badge had won!

Carl clapped Russell on the shoulder. "I'm proud of you anyway, and you should be proud, too."

"You know, it's funny," Russell said. "All I wanted was to win, but now that I've lost, I don't feel so bad about it. I got to learn all about something I love with you, and that's worth way more than winning a contest. Besides, building a roller coaster sounds like fun. . . . I can't wait to earn that badge!"

The Riley and Bing Bong Band

Riley and her imaginary friend, Bing Bong, loved making music together. Riley was good at many instruments, and nobody could play a nose like Bing Bong.

The Riley and Bing Bong Band was Joy's favorite! But the other Emotions weren't such big fans.

Anger thought the music was way too loud.

Fear kept a close eye on the instruments. One wrong move and Riley could swallow the kazoo!

Sadness only liked the minor chords, of course.

And just the sight of Bing Bong playing his nose made Disgust cringe.

One day, after playing some new tunes, Riley and Bing Bong took a break.

"We should go on tour!" said Riley.

"Great idea! Where should we go?" asked Bing Bong.

"How about Australia?" said Riley. "We can take our rocket!"

"Wooo-hooo!" exclaimed Joy.
"A new adventure!"
"We'll get homesick,"
said Sadness.

Fear gathered information
on Australia. "Koalas,
wallabies, goannas! Look at
those claws."

"Ugh! I can't. . . . I just can't,"
said Disgust.

Anger brightened when
he saw a picture of kangaroos
boxing. "Do they really box?
I'm liking this!"

"We're going to Australia," announced Riley to Mom and Dad.

"Be back for dinner," said Mom. "I'm making my famous mashed potatoes."

"Don't forget there's a big ocean between Minnesota and Australia," said Dad.

Riley whispered to Bing Bong. "We'd better bring our floaties."

"It's not a big ocean, it's a GIGANTIC ocean!" screamed Fear as he and the other Emotions looked at a map.

"Awesome!" sang Joy.

"Yeah, great. Salty air and humidity . . ." Disgust rolled her eyes. "Frizz City."

"Ohhh," groaned Sadness. "What if we get lost out there?"

"We could always become pirates!" Anger said.

Riley and Bing Bong packed up everything they needed and climbed into the rocket, preparing for liftoff.

Riley turned to Bing Bong. "Okay, copilot. Ready to check all systems?"

"Check," said Bing Bong, pointing at the controls. "Check, check, and . . . check!"

"Activating rocket booster," said Riley. "Mission Control, all systems are go!"

Riley and Bing Bong began the countdown. "Ten, nine, eight, seven, six, five, four, three, two, one . . . BLAST OFF!"

But nothing happened.

Riley and Bing Bong were confused.

"Of course!" said Riley. "The rocket can't fly without fuel!"

Riley and Bing Bong smiled at each other and began to sing their special song.

"Who's your friend who likes to play?"

The rocket answered back, binging and bonging.

Then it rumbled and roared as it flew out the window!

As they soared over the ocean, Riley and Bing Bong saw a shark, a sea turtle, a walrus, and penguins. So far, this was the best trip ever!

Suddenly, Bing Bong noticed the water was getting closer. "Are we landing?" he asked.

Riley and Bing Bong screamed as the rocket fell toward the big, blue ocean!

Riley grabbed the radio. "Mission Control, we have a problem!"

"It's over!" shouted Fear, hiding his head inside a paper bag.

"I knew it," said Sadness.

"The fuel," said Joy. "We were so busy being excited, we forgot to sing!" She plugged in an idea bulb.

"We have to sing!" shouted Riley.

"I'm so scared! I can't remember the words!" said Bing Bong.

"Sing the song! *Sing the song!*" shouted Anger.

"Sing, or we'll smell like seaweed!" yelled Disgust.

Riley shouted out the words as the rocket sputtered.

Bing Bong joined her, and the two sang louder and faster than ever before.

"Who's your friend who likes to play?

Bing Bong, Bing Bong!

His rocket makes you yell, 'Hooray!'

Bing Bong! Bing Bong!"

The rocket skimmed the surface of the ocean and then lifted back into the air! Riley and Bing Bong kept singing as the rocket soared.

Soon they could see land.
"Australia!" shouted Riley.
The Emotions cheered.

The creatures Down Under welcomed Riley and Bing Bong with big smiles.
"Play us a tune, mates," said a koala.
Riley and Bing Bong played all their songs, and the crowd went wild!
Suddenly, a familiar smell drifted through the air. "Mom's famous mashed
potatoes," Riley whispered to Bing Bong. "It's time to go home."

They played one last song and then said good-bye to their new friends and rocketed back to Minnesota.

"It's nice to be home," said Sadness.

"Sure, it's nice to be home, but traveling is so cool!" said Joy.

"I beg to differ," said Fear. "I like staying right here in good ol' Minnesota. No more trips for this guy."

"So . . . how was Australia?" asked Dad.

"It was great!" said Riley. "Tomorrow we're going on another trip—to play for the penguins in Antarctica."

"Yes!" Joy shouted.

"Noooooooooooo!" Fear screamed before he fainted onto the floor.

A Delicious Duo

Alfredo Linguini walked into his restaurant one morning to the smell of a delicious mushroom-and-cheese omelet. He entered the kitchen to find his friend Remy cooking up a wonderful breakfast for the two of them.

"What a great surprise. This looks really good!" Linguini said happily.

As they ate, Remy noticed his friend was quieter than usual. He nudged Linguini's elbow and gave him a worried look.

Linguini sighed. "Ah, it's nothing. It's just that this breakfast surprise reminded me that today is Colette's birthday, and I have no idea what to get her. Maybe some flowers? Or ah . . . a hat or—"

Remy shook his head and ran over to the stove. He thought that he and Linguini could make Colette a nice meal for her birthday, so he pretended to cook an omelet to try to make Linguini understand.

But Linguini did *not* understand. "Yeah, I already said the food was great," he said.

Remy abandoned the empty frying pan and instead picked up his favorite cookbook and tried to bring it to the table. But the book slipped from his paws and fell to the ground with a loud thud!

"Whoa!" Linguini jumped up from the table to see what had happened. "Hey, this book gave me an idea. I can *cook* her something! I bet she'd love that!"

Remy sighed with relief, glad that Linguini had figured out the perfect birthday plan.

Linguini flipped through the cookbook, shaking his head at all the fancy recipes. Finally, he landed on something he thought even *he* could cook: *scoglio*, a seafood pasta.

"What about this?" Linguini asked his friend.

Remy nodded enthusiastically and began running around the kitchen collecting the ingredients they'd need to make the dish. Whatever he didn't find in the kitchen, Linguini wrote down on a piece of paper to take to the supermarket and fish market.

Linguini also added a note to get flowers. He thought that idea was pretty good, too.

Once Linguini had the final list, he headed for the door. "Thanks for your help, Little Chef. I'll be back soon!"

But Remy jumped up onto his ladder, trying to stop Linguini before he could leave the kitchen.

Linguini shook his head. "Look, I really appreciate all your help making this list and getting ingredients, but since this is a special gift from me to Colette, I think I, uh, I want to do this on my own."

But when he got to the
supermarket, he looked down
at the list and saw that there
were *ten* ingredients needed . . .
just for the pasta sauce! With a
sigh, Linguini headed down the
closest aisle, and saw the aisle
had tons of premade jars of pasta
sauce. He knew Remy would
never approve, but with so little
time, he grabbed a sauce that
looked like the recipe picture
and moved on.

FROZEN FOODS

Next on the list was vegetables. He remembered that the cookbook
instructions listed steps for chopping and dicing and spiralizing, so he
was happy to find a freezer full of precut veggies. Linguini grabbed
some bags and headed for the checkout line.

After the supermarket, Linguini headed for the fish market and flower stand by the river.

The list said to buy fresh fish and provided a few options: mussels, scallops, shrimp. But while Linguini was deciding, he spotted a sign advertising live lobsters. *That's as fresh as fish can get!* Linguini thought. Five minutes later, he had bought the largest lobster at the fish market, quickly grabbed a bouquet of flowers, and was on his way!

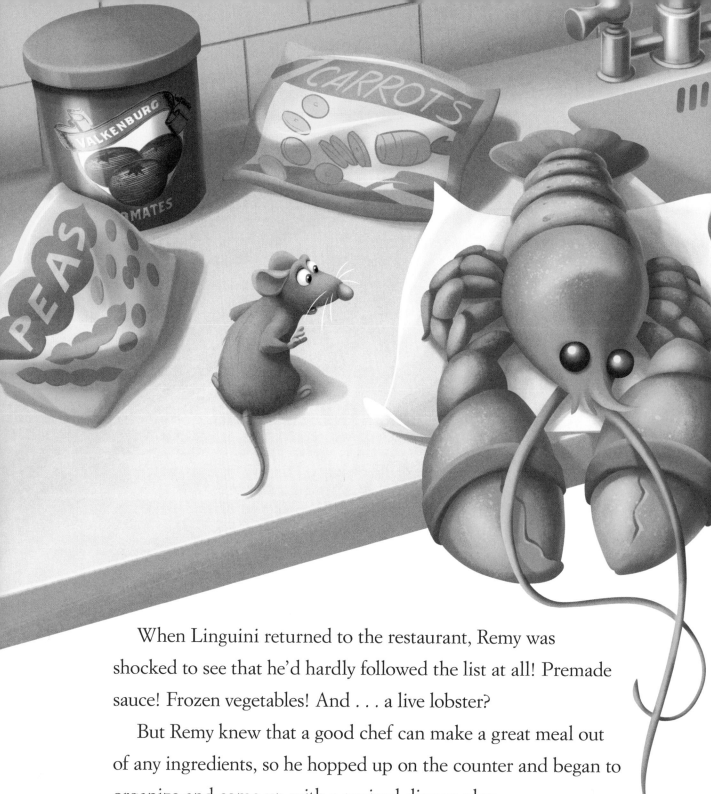

When Linguini returned to the restaurant, Remy was shocked to see that he'd hardly followed the list at all! Premade sauce! Frozen vegetables! And . . . a live lobster?

But Remy knew that a good chef can make a great meal out of any ingredients, so he hopped up on the counter and began to organize and come up with a revised dinner plan.

"Whoa, whoa, whoa, what are you doing?" Linguini asked when he noticed Remy about to open a bag of frozen veggies. "I've got it from here. Why don't you sit down and, uh, relax?"

Linguini quickly got to work on the meal. He sliced bread and put it in the oven, put the lobster in some water in a pot on the stove, and began heating the veggies in the pasta sauce. Half an hour into cooking, Linguini was a little surprised everything was going so smoothly—that was, until he turned around to see Remy testing the sauce.

"Little Chef!" Linguini exclaimed. "Have you been helping this whole time?"

Remy nodded. Linguini held out his hand, and Remy hopped onto his palm.

"I know you're just trying to help, but I *really* want to do this by myself. It's a special gift from *me* to Colette, you know? I just want to try."

Understanding, Remy headed out the kitchen door. Linguini was trying to do something from the heart, and Remy wanted to let his friend do just that.

With Remy gone, Linguini tried his best to pay extra close attention to what he was doing . . . but things quickly fell apart.

After only ten minutes, the bread was burnt, the lobster was still swimming around because he had forgotten to actually turn on the stove, and he realized he didn't buy the right pasta.

Just when Linguini thought things couldn't get any worse, the sauce exploded all over the kitchen!

Linguini sank to the floor and called for his friend. "Little Chef!"
Remy ran into the kitchen and sat down next to Linguini.

"I'm sorry, pal. I wanted this gift to be from me to her, but I think
we'll create something even more special together. Would you help
me finish cooking? Colette deserves a great meal on her birthday, and
I know with your help *we* can make one."

Remy got up and began running around the kitchen looking for anything he could save from the sauce explosion. Then he started flipping through the cookbook, searching for a different recipe.

Eventually, Remy found something they could make together using what Linguini had left from the store and what Remy had in the restaurant. He hopped on Linguini's head to get to work. But first he and Linguini moved the lobster back into its tank. They'd set the little guy free later.

Just as they finished cooking, Colette arrived at the restaurant.

Linguini led her to a table, where Remy had set the food and the flowers. "Linguini by Linguini . . . and Little Chef!" he announced proudly.

"This food smells amazing!" she exclaimed, smiling. "And how'd you know this was my favorite pasta growing up? And flowers, too!"

Linguini and Remy shared a knowing look.

"I had a bit of help," Linguini chuckled. "Happy birthday, Colette."

Teaming Up

When Mike Wazowski was a young monster, his class visited Monsters, Inc., where the top Scarers in Monstropolis worked. These monsters went through special doors into the human world to collect screams from human children. Then the screams were changed into energy for the town.

During the trip, Mike snuck through an open door and watched as a Scarer made a child scream. That's when Mike decided he wanted to be a Scarer when he grew up.

Mike worked hard until he was accepted to Monsters University! On the first day of college, Mike's bus pulled up in front of the gates of a beautiful old campus. "Wow," Mike breathed. He checked out the clubs and something called the Scare Games, a contest in which students competed to see who was scariest.

On the first day of class, Mike went to Scaring 101.

"Who can tell me the principles of an effective roar?" Professor Knight asked.

Mike started to answer. But just then—

"ROAAAAAR!" Another monster surprised everyone.

The monster who had roared was named James P. Sullivan. His friends called him Sulley. Scaring came easily to him, so he never studied. He was only interested in having fun and goofing off. His grades showed it.

Mike, on the other hand, studied every night. He read every book on scaring and practiced his scare techniques. He didn't want to fail his final exam. If he did, he'd be out of the Scaring Program.

On the day of the scaring final, Mike and Sulley began to argue. Then they got into a roaring face-off. Everyone was watching, including the head of the School of Scaring, Dean Hardscrabble.

Sulley accidentally knocked over a scream can. It held the record-breaking scream Dean Hardscrabble had collected in her scaring days.

The canister hit the floor. *"Ahhhhhhhhhhhhhhhhhh!"*

Hardscrabble's scream was gone.

"I am so sorry!" cried Mike.

"It was an accident!" insisted Sulley.

Dean Hardscrabble proceeded to give Mike and Sulley their final exams, and she was not impressed. She decided neither would be continuing in the Scaring Program. Sulley was speechless and stormed out of the room.

Hardscrabble turned to Mike. "Mr. Wazowski, what you lack is something that can't be taught. You're not scary."

Mike was crushed.

The next semester, Mike and Sulley were put in the Scream Can Design Program. They were miserable . . . until Mike remembered the Scare Games.

Dean Hardscrabble made a deal with Mike. "If you win, I'll let your entire team into the Scaring Program. But if you lose, you will leave Monsters University."

All he had to do was find a fraternity to join so he could compete.

There was only one option: Oozma Kappa, a group of misfits who weren't exactly scary.

The problem was Oozma Kappa needed one more member.

"The star player has just arrived," Sulley told Mike.

Mike was not happy, but he had no choice. He and Sulley
moved into the Oozma Kappa house and met Don, Art, Squishy,
Terri, and Terry.

In the opening event of the Scare Games, the first team to make it through a tunnel of stinging glow urchins would win. The last would be out.

Mike and Sulley tied for second. But they'd left the rest of their team behind, so Oozma Kappa came in last. Luckily, another team was disqualified. Oozma Kappa was still in the games!

Oozma Kappa made it through the next challenge, too, but everyone except Mike and Sulley wanted to quit. "We're built for other things," Don explained.

So Mike decided to take the gang on a field trip to Monsters, Inc. While there, Mike realized something. "There's no one type of Scarer. The best Scarers use their differences to their advantage."

Mike and Sulley admitted they'd been acting like jerks. "We could be a great team," Mike said. "We just need to start working together."

The next morning, Mike and Sulley felt inspired! They woke up bright and early and leaped out of bed.

They trained the OKs in everything they would need to know for the next two events: how to scare kids and avoid teenagers, how to hide, and even how to do scary feet drills to make sure everyone was in tip-top condition.

Oozma Kappa was even more determined to win. They made it through the Don't Scare the Teen and the Hide and Sneak events. They were finally a team . . . and, even better, they were friends.

But that night Sulley ran into Dean Hardscrabble. "Tomorrow each of you must prove you're undeniably scary," she said, "and I know for a fact that one of you is not."

Sulley knew she was talking about Mike. Mike was smart, talented, and the hardest-working monster he'd ever met! But he was also small, friendly, and not exactly scary.

Sulley was worried. He really wanted his team to win—and the next day was the final Scare Games event.

The big day arrived. There were just two fraternities left: Roar Omega Roar and Oozma Kappa.

The monsters had to scare a robot child. One by one, the members of both teams faced off. In the end, it came down to Mike.

"Rooooooooooar!" He got a perfect score. Oozma Kappa had won the Scare Games!

But Mike soon discovered that Sulley had cheated. He'd changed the setting to "easy" during Mike's turn. "You don't think I'm scary?"

"What was I supposed to do? Let the whole team fail?" Sulley replied.

Mike wanted to
prove he *was* scary. He
snuck through a door into the human world and ended
up in a camp cabin filled with dangerous children. But they
didn't think he was scary, either.

Sulley snuck through the door to get his friend back. But Mike wanted
Sulley to leave. After what had happened, Mike didn't think he was special.

"I try to give people what they want, but all I do is let them down,"
Sulley told Mike. "You're not the only failure here."

Mike was surprised.

But just then, the rangers arrived.

Mike and Sulley knew they needed to get back to the monster world. To open the door, Sulley had to scare the rangers enough to power the door.

When Mike and Sulley made it back to Monsters University, they were kicked out of school. They hugged the OKs good-bye and left for their next big adventure together . . . in the mailroom at Monsters, Inc.!

DISNEY · PIXAR

WALL·E

Back on Earth

After the *Axiom* landed back on Earth, the Captain wanted to help all the passengers and robots aboard the ship adjust to the changes life on the planet would bring. He knew that by working together, they could all make Earth their home . . . even after having only lived on a luxury spaceship in outer space.

WALL·E was happy to be back on Earth and even happier not to be lonely anymore. He watched his favorite movies with EVE, collected even more new treasures with his robot friends, and still tidied up the planet—one piece of trash at a time.

But EVE was having a harder time finding something to do on Earth. Her original directive was to scan the planet for any sign of plant life . . . and she'd found it. Now she wasn't sure how to fill her days. So she just flew around, still scanning and scanning and scanning.

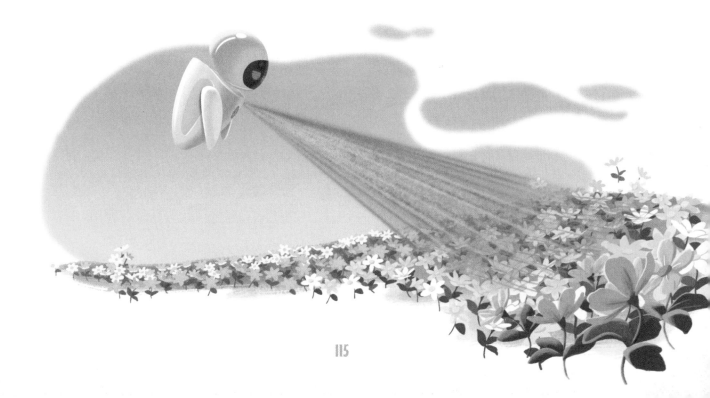

One day, the Captain noticed EVE wandering around aimlessly.
He had to help her somehow. The Captain went to WALL·E, hoping
that together they'd find a new purpose perfectly suited for EVE.

"I want everyone to feel at home and be happy here, WALL·E. But EVE seems like she's looking for something. Can you help?" he asked.

WALL·E beeped in agreement. He quickly rolled home to come up with a plan to cheer EVE up.

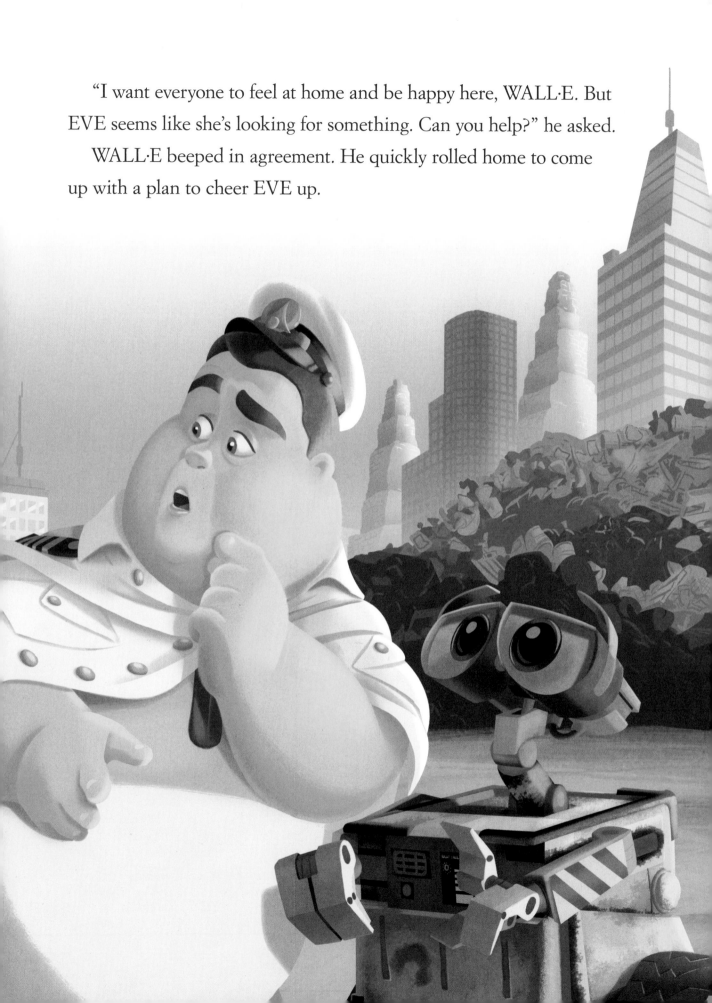

After a few days of thinking it over, WALL·E had the perfect idea: he would give EVE her very own one-of-a-kind garden!

EVE already knew how to find plant life, but maybe now she could make plant life grow. And even better, all their robot friends could help. He knew EVE would love her garden even more if it was something they created together.

WALL·E thought his friends could first help by clearing the land around his house. They removed rocks, roots, sticks, and trash from the soil, making sure it was perfect for whatever EVE wanted to grow.

Then WALL·E built a fence around the piece of land using his compacted-trash units.

Next his friends helped him gather some supplies. EVE would need seeds, plant bulbs, and gardening tools.

When the time finally came to show EVE what they had made, WALL·E could barely contain his excitement.

He asked EVE to close her eyes, and he led her to the newly enclosed piece of land. When they arrived, he beeped for her to open her eyes.

WALL·E told EVE that this garden was hers to take care of. She stared in amazement before she got to thinking and then got to work! She even assigned some jobs to her friends.

EVE thought VAQ-M would be perfect at planting seeds. WALL·E drilled holes into a large patch of dirt, and EVE gave some seeds to VAQ-M. Moments later, VAQ-M sneezed them right into the holes WALL·E had made.

In the corner, EVE was planting some flowers and vegetables that needed less sun than the rest of the garden. She knew exactly which umbrella-bot could help!

BRL-A could open his canopy and guard the plants from the sun as they started to grow.

EVE thought M-O would be able to help her clean the fruits and vegetables. Since he wanted to clean up *all* the dirt *all* the time, she knew he'd be delighted to help.

And he was! "Foreign contaminants!" M-O cheered.

Then EVE walked VN-GO to the fence WALL·E had built. VN-GO was ecstatic to find a blank canvas to showcase his art. Even if the paint splashed everywhere, it still made the little boxes of trash look more beautiful.

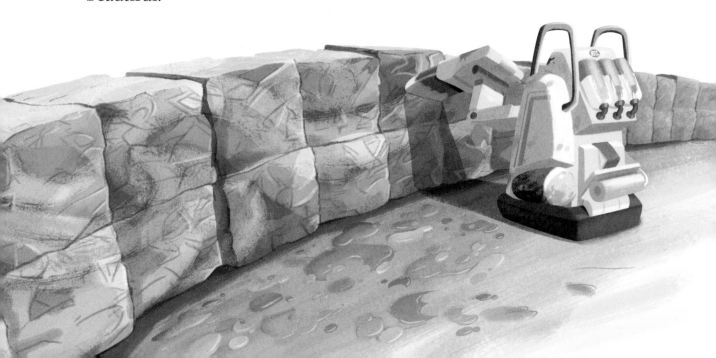

A few days later, the Captain visited WALL·E and EVE's home to check on their progress. He was thrilled to see WALL·E's plan had worked. Building and managing a garden really was the perfect job for EVE! She looked happier than he'd seen her since they had returned to Earth.

But then he noticed EVE flying back and forth—and then back and forth again—with a watering can.

Hmmm . . . he thought.

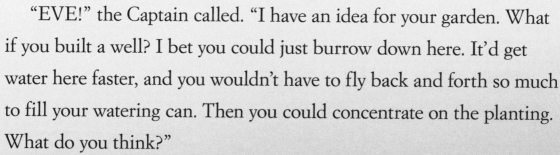

"EVE!" the Captain called. "I have an idea for your garden. What if you built a well? I bet you could just burrow down here. It'd get water here faster, and you wouldn't have to fly back and forth so much to fill your watering can. Then you could concentrate on the planting. What do you think?"

EVE beeped excitedly. She *loved* the idea!

For the first time back on Earth, EVE felt like she had a new directive. Over time, her garden grew and grew. It wasn't long before EVE and WALL·E had gardens surrounding their home.

"WALL·E!" EVE beeped happily. Her gardens became her favorite places on Earth. She loved spending time surrounded by her plants, with her favorite robot by her side.

The Rivera Family Band

The Rivera shoe workshop was full of exciting sounds. All three cousins had an upcoming celebration on their minds as they turned their tools into musical instruments.

"Only one more day until Día de los Muertos!" said Abel.

"Yep!" said Miguel with a grin. "And tomorrow is the talent show in Mariachi Plaza, too!" He had the best idea for that year. "What if our family performs together . . . in a band?"

Meanwhile, in the Land of the Dead, someone else was having the very same idea.

"What if," Mamá Imelda pondered, "for this year's Día de los Muertos, all the Riveras perform together in the Land of the Living?"

"How will we know where to go? Or what to play?" said Tío Oscar.

Mamá Coco laughed. "There's a talent show in Mariachi Plaza. Miguel performed in it last year, and something tells me he'll be there again."

"As for the songs," said Mamá Imelda with a sly grin, "I think he'll choose one by our very own Héctor."

Back in Santa Cecilia, the cousins' workday finally comes to a close. They headed outside to talk things over.

"We've never performed in front of an audience," said Rosa.

"What if we mess up?" added Abel.

"Don't worry about that," Miguel replied. "This isn't for them. It's for us. It's a chance to honor the music that's in our blood."

Meanwhile, in the Land of the Dead, Héctor was absolutely thrilled. "I think performing together will be fun. Especially now that music has returned to our family."

"Exactamente," said Mamá Imelda, catching Héctor's gaze. "That's exactly what I was thinking."

"It's going to be awesome," Miguel said. "We'll be onstage together, playing the same songs we always do!"

But Rosa and Abel were still a bit uneasy. "I don't know, Miguel," said Rosa.

"I understand," Miguel said. "I was scared the first time I performed. But if we practice, it might help calm your nerves."

Miguel, Abel, and Rosa slowly started to play their instruments, and eventually, the cousins found their groove. The music wasn't perfect, but they were having a great time.

"Miguel, what's going on here?" asked Abuelita, interrupting the rehearsal. Socorro giggled while Mamá and Papá followed.

Miguel stood up, waving his guitar. "We're starting a music group—the Rivera Family Band! I want the whole family to perform together tomorrow at the talent show."

"I don't think so, mi hijo," said Abuelita.

Then, out of nowhere, Mamá grabbed the guitar. "I'll give it a try," she said. "I've always wanted to be a músico for a day."

Mamá struck a terrible chord and grinned. "I like this!" she said. Although she was delighted, the rest of the family was unimpressed.

"Well, that was something," said Abuelita, avoiding Mamá's gaze.
"But we should get back to preparing the ofrenda."

"Abuelita is right," said Abel. "There's no way we'll be ready in time
for the show tomorrow. Let's focus on the things we're already good at."

The family headed back into the house, leaving Miguel alone.

Miguel was frustrated. That hadn't gone as planned.

Dante—Miguel's faithful companion—barked, then nudged Miguel's guitar with his nose.

Suddenly, a thought struck Miguel: while Mamá wasn't a great musician, she had looked so happy when she was strumming the guitar. He knew Abel and Rosa enjoyed their instruments, too.

Miguel stood up with renewed determination. "Music brought our family together, and this performance is for all the Riveras!"

Meanwhile, in the Land of the Dead, Mamá Imelda explained her idea. "Our music is a way of thanking our living family for remembering us and letting them know how much we still love them."

"I love to visit our family. But—" said Tío Felipe.

"The living family won't even be able to hear us play," said Tío Óscar, finishing his brother's sentence.

"That might be true," said Mamá Coco. "But the living Riveras will be able to feel our presence and our love."

"Well, I'm in," replied Tía Victoria. "It's for family!"

As the family began to rehearse, Papá Julio had a moment of sheer brilliance. "Hey! Should our band be called 'the Dead Riveras'?"

"Yes, that's perfecto!" Héctor exclaimed.

Back in the Land of the Living, Miguel followed Abuelita into the ofrenda room. He knew that if he could convince her to join, the rest of the family would, too.

To Miguel's surprise, Abuelita was singing to Socorro.

"Abuelita," Miguel said, "you've *got* to be part of our band for the talent show!"

"Not again, mi hijo," Abuelita said, shaking her head.

"Please," Miguel said. "For Mamá Coco and all the Riveras. It's a way of remembering our family."

Abuelita was still conflicted. "I've spent most of my life shutting out music. I don't even know how to play any instruments."

"La voz," Miguel said. "Your voice is your instrument. All you have to do is sing from the heart."

"Okay, Miguel," she said, grabbing his hand. "Let's find the rest of our family and get the band ready."

In the Land of the Dead, the Dead Riveras had found their rhythm, too, and walked over the Marigold Bridge at the same time the living Riveras walked into town with their instruments.

Abel's stomach was in knots. "I think I'm feeling a little nervous," he said.

"Don't worry, Abel," Abuelita said with a smile in her voice. "No matter what happens, we will be together. Just try to enjoy the celebration."

The Dead Riveras arrived at Mariachi Plaza to find that the living Riveras were already performing onstage.

"Look!" said Héctor, pointing at a nearby sign. "It says 'Rivera Family Band'!"

"That means us, too," said Papá Julio.

The Dead Riveras rushed the stage and joined the band. As the living and dead family members performed together, the love and joy could be felt by them all.

"This was a great idea," Héctor whispered into Mamá Imelda's ear.
She beamed. The feeling of music and love was electric. The moment
was even better than she had imagined.

In fact, it was the greatest Día de los Muertos any Rivera could
remember.

Merida's Challenge

Merida couldn't stop laughing. "You three wee bairns think you can climb the Crone's Tooth?"

The Crone's Tooth was the tallest mountain around.

"Only the biggest and bravest people have climbed it—including me," she continued. "Don't even try."

Harris, Hubert, and Hamish scowled. Of course they would give it a try! They were big and brave, too. They had to prove it to Merida.

Now, as they stood at the foot of the towering rock, Harris and
Hubert weren't so sure it was a good idea. But Hamish was ready.
He'd show Merida!

They gave him a boost, but he struggled to find handholds in
the slippery rock.

A little way up, the rock Hamish was standing on fell away. He
was left dangling . . . by his fingertips!

Harris and Hubert hurried to fetch Merida.

They found her in the castle and told her what had happened to Hamish at the Crone's Tooth.

"Och, no!" cried Merida. "What have I done? I didn't really mean you should try to climb it yourselves! Come on, we have to get Angus."

But Merida was so worried, she couldn't think straight. "Where are my arrows?" she cried to her brothers. Luckily, Hubert was one step ahead of her, and he tossed them to his sister.

When they got to Angus in the stables, Merida was still worried they wouldn't make it to the Crone's Tooth in time to save Hamish. "I'm all thumbs," Merida said. "I'll never get this bridle on!" Harris quickly helped his sister get ready to ride.

Soon they were galloping toward the Crone's Tooth.
"Faster, Angus!" Merida urged. "Faster!"

Hamish was still hanging on when they arrived . . . but barely. He kicked the wall, trying to find a foothold. Something blue caught Merida's eye. "Wisps! I should've known." She called out to her brother, "Hold on, Hamish! Please hold on!"

Merida scanned the trees around the clearing. "Quick! Harris, Hubert! Gather as many fallen leaves as you can. I have an idea!" Soon they had formed a large pile under Hamish.

Merida looped a rope around her waist and knotted it tightly. She tied the end to an arrow.

Stepping back, she sent the arrow flying over the high branch of a tree.

Then Harris hurried to fetch the arrow from the ground and tied the rope to Angus's saddle.

"Angus," Merida said, "walk up that hill."

The branch groaned as Angus pulled the rope taut. Everyone held their breath.

"Keep pulling slowly," Merida said. The branch groaned again.

The rope began to hoist Merida into the air.

Fragments of rock pattered down as Hamish began to lose his grip. "Just a wee bit longer, Hamish," yelled Merida. "Ignore those wisps!"

Finally, Merida was high enough to grab her brother. "I've got you!" Merida laughed, hugging him tightly. "Angus, you can start walking backward now."

Angus slowly lowered Merida and Hamish over the pile of leaves. When she was sure it was safe, Merida dropped Hamish on the leaves. The rescue mission was a success!

"How brave you all were," Merida said to her brothers. "You, Hamish, for hanging in there so long. And you, Harris and Hubert, for being so calm and reliable all through the rescue." But the triplets had one more thought on their minds. . . .

As the wisps flew away to cause mischief elsewhere, the brothers crossed their arms and looked to their sister.

"Okay, okay!" said Merida, laughing. "I promise I won't question your bravery again!"

You're It, Dory!

After school, Nemo, Marlin, Dory, and all their friends decided to play a game of hide-and-seek. Dory was "It" first! Everyone swam to find a hiding place as she began to count.

"One . . . two . . . three . . . um . . . four . . . um . . . um . . ." Dory counted.

When Dory opened her eyes, she forgot why she was counting!

"Hmmm, what was I about to do? Lie and sneak? No. Why would I do that? Spy and peek? No . . . that can't be right. Oh! Hide-and-seek!" she said, swimming off toward Nemo and Marlin's anemone, hoping to find them there.

But by the time Dory got to their anemone, she'd forgotten why she went. She kept swimming closer. She had a nagging feeling she shouldn't get *too* close, but she couldn't remember why. . . .

"YEEOWCH!" she exclaimed. "Now I remember. I'm not supposed to touch anemones because they sting!"

As she swam away, rubbing her stung fin, Marlin and Nemo peeked out from their anemone.

"Where's she going, Dad?" Nemo asked. "She was so close to finding us!"

"I'm not sure . . ." Marlin responded.

"Hmmm, what was I doing again?" Dory asked herself. She tried her best to remember, but she kept getting distracted and swimming right past all her friends.

"My spot is so good!" Pearl whispered to Bob after Dory swam by.

"Mine too! I love hide-and-seek!" Bob whispered back.

Dory even swam right over Mr. Ray! She was so excited to see a
large patch of pristine sand to squish and play with that she completely
missed him hiding beneath it! Mr. Ray smiled, proud of his clever
hiding place.

"Wait! Wasn't I playing hide-and-seek?" Dory said, finally remembering.

"Wow, that guy looks a lot like Hank," Dory said. "What color is he again? Yellow? No. Pink? Nope, I don't think so. Blue?"

Dory continued to swim through the coral field, and Hank tried his best to blend in with his surroundings as she got closer to him.

"That was a close call," Hank said to himself when Dory eventually swam away to seek another friend.

But as Dory swam through the Great Barrier Reef, she forgot again she was playing hide-and-seek.

She swam right past Bailey, who was hiding behind some seaweed, and even swam right *over* Destiny, who was hiding on the ocean floor!

As Dory kept swimming, she spotted a beautiful purple shell on the sand.

"My mom loves shells!" she said. "I should give this one to her. But I haven't seen my mom or dad in a while. Actually, I haven't seen any of my friends. Where are they?"

That's when Dory remembered they were playing a game of hide-and-seek . . . but not that she was "It"!

"Uh-oh, I better find a hiding spot quick!" she said.

Dory's parents, Charlie and Jenny, watched from their hiding place as Dory swam into a nearby cave. They expected her to come out once she realized no one was hiding there, but after a couple of minutes, they started to worry.

They agreed that they should go check on their daughter. Shortly after entering the cave, they found Dory.

"Kelpcake, what are you up to?" Charlie said.

"Mom! Dad! We're playing hide-and-seek, and I found this *great* hiding spot! Come in, I'll make room," Dory told them.

"But, sweetie—" Jenny tried to explain that everyone was hiding from Dory, but before she could, Dory swam to the opening of the cave.

Dory saw Hank and Mr. Ray swimming past the cave and wanted to help them hide, too. "Okay, okay, everybody in. We can squeeze," she told them.

"But, Dory—" Mr. Ray began, but before he could get another word out, Dory saw even more of her friends in need of a hiding spot.

Eventually, Dory's cave was packed. Nearly everyone who was supposed to be hiding from Dory was in the cave with her!

"It's gonna be tight," she said to her friends. "Destiny, suck it in a bit. Watch your head, Bailey!"

Finally, Nemo and Marlin wandered into the cave. They were shocked to find all their friends crowded in with Dory!

"Dory," Nemo said, "what are you doing?"

"Nemo! We are . . . hmmm . . . What *are* we doing?"

"Playing hide-and-seek!" everyone shouted.

The group swam out of the cave as Nemo explained what had happened.

"But you're 'It,' Dory. You're supposed to be looking for *us*."

"Oh, I see. . . . Found you!" Dory exclaimed.

Marlin had a solution. "Let's just play tag."

INCREDIBLES 2
Babysitting Mode

Fashion designer Edna Mode wasn't thrilled when Bob Parr, better known as Mr. Incredible, asked her to babysit his son Jack-Jack. Edna simply wasn't good with babies.

But Jack-Jack was no *ordinary* baby. As soon as his dad left, Jack-Jack began to float! Edna was delighted, and she wondered what else he could do.

Edna knew that each Super was unique . . . but there was something extra special about little Jack-Jack. "Okay, little one," she said. "I am ready. Thrill me with your prowess!" Edna wanted to observe him and take notes for his next supersuit design.

But where is my sketchbook? she wondered.

There was no time to find it, though—Jack-Jack was on the move!

Edna couldn't believe Jack-Jack could walk right through a wall. "You are simply amazing, *dahling*!" Edna said as she watched him. The little boy could not be stopped! He continued to pass in and out of the walls as he floated down the hallway.

Suddenly, Jack-Jack disappeared right before her eyes!

Where in the world can that little boy be? Edna wondered as she searched. *I mustn't forget to put a tracking device in his supersuit.*

"Come out, come out, *dahling*," she called.

Edna looked high and low, behind furniture and in every room, but Jack-Jack was nowhere to be found.

Finally, Edna found Jack-Jack downstairs, near her lab. The Super baby smiled and pointed at his new discovery . . .

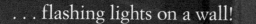

. . . flashing lights on a wall!

Jack-Jack had found the security system for Edna's testing room. The alarm began to beep loudly at him!

In the blink of an eye, he morphed into a pint-sized Edna, and the alarm stopped immediately. The security system thought Jack-Jack was actually Edna!

Edna marveled at the
miniature version of herself.
She had truly never seen
anything so extraordinary.

Once inside Edna's lab, little Jack-Jack discovered some of the supersuits Edna had designed. He couldn't wait to get his hands on the colorful costumes, and he immediately started trying on bits and pieces of many different ones. He tried on gloves and masks, and even fashioned a cape for himself.

But Edna quickly shared her one and only design rule: NO CAPES!

But Jack-Jack absolutely loved the cape he had created, and he did not want to take it off. He got so angry that he turned into a little monster! Edna didn't panic, though—she was used to working with Supers of all kinds.

Edna knew that little monster Jack-Jack meant it was time for his bottle.

How can I calm him down long enough to feed him? she wondered. Then Edna had an idea, and she headed to her music room. Maybe the right song would help Jack-Jack change back into a baby . . . and keep him from destroying all her favorite records.

Edna played Beethoven for the little monster. It worked! He
transformed back into an adorable baby.

But suddenly, ONE Jack-Jack multiplied into TWO . . .
THREE . . . FOUR . . . FIVE Jack-Jacks!

There was no way Edna could feed five hungry Jack-Jacks
with just one bottle!

So Edna switched the music from Beethoven to Mozart. Success! All the Jack-Jacks merged back into one baby. He began to giggle as he watched his bottle heat up on the stove, and then . . . *WHOOOOSH!* Jack-Jack burst into flames!

Still, Edna remained calm—she had seen it ALL!

After putting out Jack-Jack's flames, Edna finally spotted her sketchbook.

But it was hard to design a supersuit for Jack-Jack when he kept destroying her pencils with his laser beam eyes!

She tried to keep him busy with his bottle so she could return to sketching.

"Teleportation . . . telekinesis . . . laser vision . . . phase shifting . . . That is all I need to see!" Edna said as she started to create his brand-new supersuit.

Later that evening, Edna told Jack-Jack a story about the adventures of his family, the Incredibles, and their heroic little boy—who, of course, used his amazing powers to save the day!

With a full belly and a smile on his face, Jack-Jack drifted off to sleep.

"Good night, *dahling*," Edna said to the little one.

The next morning, Jack-Jack saw Bob's arrival on the monitor. "Dada . . ." Jack-Jack said, pointing to the screen.

"Yes, Dada is here," Edna said, walking Jack-Jack to Bob's car. "Let's go show him how fabulous you look."

When they got there, Bob said to Edna, "Thanks again, E, for everything. How much do I owe you?"

"Pishposh, *dahling*. Babysitting this one," said Edna, "I do for free."